Francis Gentleman

The General

A poem - Respectfully inscribed to the Right Honourable the Marquis of

Granby

Francis Gentleman

The General
A poem - Respectfully inscribed to the Right Honourable the Marquis of Granby

ISBN/EAN: 9783337196370

Printed in Europe, USA, Canada, Australia, Japan

Cover: Foto ©Andreas Hilbeck / pixelio.de

More available books at **www.hansebooks.com**

THE

GENERAL.

A

P O E M.

Respectfully inscribed to the Right Honourable the

Marquis of GRANBY.

By the AUTHOR of

A T R I P to the M O O N.

———*nequeo monstrare, et sentio tantum.* Juv.
'Tis what I feel, yet strive in vain to show.

L O N D O N:

Printed for W. NICOLL, and W. BRISTOW, in *St. Paul's Church-Yard*;
and C. ETHERINGTON, in *York.*
MDCCLXIV.

GENERAL.

IMMORTAL Shade! of each immortal Name!
    That ſhines recorded in the Liſts of *Fame*;
Not thoſe who from hereditary Light,
With the falſe Glare of borrow'd Beams are bright;
But ſuch as Merit with rich Blood combine,
Reflecting Honour on a Noble Line;
That like the *Phœnix*, with peculiar Grace,
Unſtain'd preſerve the Beauties of their Race.
If the frail Buſtle of this tranſient State
With immaterial Spirits can have Weight,
From thoſe *Ætherial* Manſions where you reſt,
Star-crown'd, in Pomp of virtuous Glory bleſt,

B   Propitious

Propitious come—an honeſt Muſe inſpire—
Nerve her weak Wing—lend *your* heroic Fire—
With your undaunted Ardour lead her on,
And teach her, *Eagle-like*, to view the Sun:
None but the Bird of JOVE ſhould tempt a Flight,
That ruſhes on a Blaze of cloudleſs Light.

Firſt, JUSTICE come with thy impartial Scale,
Leſt *Prejudice* or *Int'reſt* ſhould prevail;
Take from *Reflection* ev'ry Power of Thought,
Ere that a ſingle Compliment be *bought*;
Shield *Reaſon*'s Eye with thy protecting Hand,
From the dread Influence of PACTOLIAN Sand;
Which, ſcatter'd by *Corruption* as ſhe flies,
Pretending Patriots choaks—or dims their Eyes;
Corruption, who, as MIDAS could of old,
With magic Touch turns any Thing to Gold,
Locks up the Senſes, or inverts their Power,
Melting the hardeſt Heart with DANAE's Show'r.
Nor yet let pois'nous Rage her Venom ſpit,
Satire run mad is the *Buffoon* of Wit;
From whoſe foul Mouth no Character's ſecure,
That lays the Baſtard Vice at any Door;

That-

That prays or curfes, wheedles or knocks down,
Urg'd by that powerful Motive—*Half a Crown.*

Wither fuch *Bays*—if any *Bays* can rife
Beneath the Influence of fuch churlifh Skies;
Where no mild Gleams of Summer cheer the Plain,
But Storms, and everlafting Winter reign;
Bays which, like *Nightfhade*, fcatter Poifon round,
Infect the circling Air—profane the Ground;
Call forth *Deftruction* from her dark Abodes,
And with fell Venom fwell ten thoufand Toads.

Honeft may CHURCHILL be, for ought I know,
Some Lines depict him, and I wifh him fo:
Let him enjoy his Profit and his Praife,
In thefe fo politic and gen'rous Days;
Let him fuccefsfully purfue his Plan,
And prey upon the tend'reft Part of Man;
Blufhlefs, remorfelefs, and without Control,
Plunder *th' immediate Jewel of the Soul:*
Let him, *Humanity* thrown quite afide,
Indulge his Spleen, his Int'reft, or his Pride;
Let him in *Scandal* wade thro' Thick and Thin,
To praife each *Out*—and cenfure ev'ry *In :*

Let

Let him, to pleafe a Crowd of Knaves and Fools,
Paint MONARCHS, or their MINISTERS, as Tools:
Let him, ftill more to proftitute the MUSE,
A neighb'ring Nation by the *Lump* abufe:
Let him, in boundlefs Rage, pronounce the Lot
Of blackeft Infamy to ev'ry SCOT:
Let him, like Humankind's imperial * Foe,
Wifh to behead them at a fingle Blow:
Let him, if not content to rail at home,
O'er the fubmiffive World's wide Limits roam;
Fit to engage a fingle Foe or Hoft,
Ready to fight a NABOB or a *Ghoft:*
From Clime to Clime Malevolence transfer,
Diftinguifh'd—*Nature's Executioner.*
All this, as gracious *Heav'n* in Mercy fends
Plagues to perplex us for peculiar Ends,
With Patience will we bear—but let him paufe—
Nor longer dare, in raging *Party*'s Caufe,
(*Party*, of whom it may be juftly faid,
Behold a Monfter! without Heart or Head,
By Madnefs, Av'rice, Pride, and Jealoufy,
Ingender'd on the Snake-lock'd Sifters three,
While Tyrant *Satire* waves her bloody Rod)
So oft to trifle with an awful GOD.

* *Caligula.*

That

That GOD whofe Service to become a *Wit*,
The *Rev'rend* BARD moft pioufly hath quit;
And why? Becaufe—Oh Reafon moft divine—
His narrow Income could not purchafe *Wine*.
That GOD, who, were he cruel to this Earth,
As *Men* to *Men* for Profit are or Mirth,
With fportive Thunder would confound the whole,
Nor fpare e'en mighty CHURCHILL's *Patriot* Soul.

Think not, miftaken Bard, I am thy Foe,
I neither know thee, nor can wifh to know:
Reflected in thy Works thy Mind I view,
And grieve to find it of a Sable Hue:
Strong Beams of *Genius* gild the STYGIAN Gloom,
And *fancy* Webs there in her fineft Loom;
Expreffion well arrays her verbal Band,
And *Judgment* leads them with a Mafter Hand;
While JANUS-fronted Int'reft flily waves
A flaming Banner to all Party Slaves;
Whofe gaudy Hieroglyphics catch the Eye,
A poor fantaftic Shade of *Liberty*.
This Patch-work Medley, blending Right and Wrong,
An impious, moral, foothing, fneering Song,

That shows the tortur'd *Muse* in various State,
Now bred at *Court*, now fresh from *Billingsgate*,
May cheat the Sensible, or charm the Rude,
May steal or thunder through the Multitude.

For my poor Part, by various Passions wrought,
I praise the Numbers while I damn the Thought;
I weep to see such Flights of Golden Darts,
With deadly Poison tipp'd, to rankle Hearts;
And, while the lovely Snake-like Verse I scan,
Praise crowns the *Bard*—while Censure marks the *Man.*

What has provok'd this unknown Scribe, you'll say,
This feeble, nameless Mushroom of a Day;
This unfledg'd Rhimer to attempt a Flight,
When such a *Falcon Muse* appears in Sight?
What could induce the unimpassion'd Elf,
Who wishes me unfeeling as himself;
What Motives have arous'd the slumb'ring Drone,
Thus to assault me on *Satiric* Throne?
Me! Me! a Monosyllable of Weight,
To give a thousand grov'ling Reptiles Fate;
Can such a lifeless and insipid Thing
E'er hope to pierce me with his feeble Sting?

As

As well a Bee, that hunts the flow'ry Field,
Might ftrive to wound thro' AJAX' feven-fold Shield:
Mankind muft ridicule fo dull an Ass,
Who breaks his Hoof againft a *Front* of *Brafs*.

Some Water-drinking Sprite—for gen'rous *Wine*
Would make a native Blockhead brighter fhine:
Wine which he fneers at in his tart Reproof,
As turning *poor* Divinity aloof:
With my own Weapons dares my pond'rous Rage,
A DAVID to GOLIAH on the Stage.

Well haft thou pictur'd my unequal Force,
But think *that* DAVID check'd the GIANT's Courfe;
I own thee Proof 'gainft all Attacks of Shame,
Plung'd over Head and Ears in SHANNON's * Stream;
But haft thou too with great ACHILLES try'd
The mighty Pow'r of STYX's awful Tide?
Is there no Spot wherein to make thee feel?
Yes, CONSCIENCE will convert thee all to Heel.

To pleafe no *Patron*, nor to grafp at *Pelf*,
Slave to no *Party*—I oppofe myfelf:

Free

* A River in *Ireland*, whofe Water is faid to blefs thofe dipp'd in it with invincible Affurance.

Free by my Birth, ftill freer by my Heart,
Of injur'd Humankind I take the Part;
Boldly I ftand 'gainft *Paffion*'s dang'rous Sway,
And with cool *Wifdom* take the Middle Way;
Yet not fo cold, but, for my Country's Good,
In Danger's Onfet I could fpill my Blood;
Give freely my poor All to aid her Caufe,
To guard her KING, and, guarding him, her LAWS.

    With Generofity and Friendfhip fir'd,
Why may not bounteous TEMPLE be admir'd?
TEMPLE! whofe Principles reflected fhow
The Richnefs, Tafte, and Elegance of STOWE.
Tho' diff'ring Statefmen may explode his Aim,
Why may not DEVONSHIRE true Glory claim?
Whofe fteady Temper, and whofe honeft Heart,
Are nobly form'd to act a *Patriot* Part.
May we not fafely honour and commend
In ROCKINGHAM a BRUNSWICK's faithful Friend?
WENTWORTH! whofe Virtues act without Controul,
Not more a Lord in Title than in Soul:
WENTWORTH! whofe Noble Deeds his Mind approve;
WENTWORTH! whom Men and *Liberty* muft Love.

                                        Of

Of filver-hair'd NEWCASTLE kindly fing,
A well-defigning Servant of his KING,
Tho' now, perhaps, o'erpow'r'd with num'rous Years,
Unfit to bear a Nation's cumb'rous Cares.

Hating, like SWIFT, a BISHOP for his Place,
Can we no Beauties in a DRUMMOND trace?
Shall modeft *Truth* reftrain her honeft Tongue,
And leave him in the undiftinguifh'd Throng?
A *Prelate* by his *Virtues* dignify'd,
Juft without Rigour, awful without Pride;
Pious without enthufiaftic Flame,
All that fheds Luftre on a facred Name,
Shines Rev'rend YORK——compleat in ev'ry Senfe,
Religion's Pride, and Boaft of *Eloquence.*

Why fhould we fear to fpeak a SAVILE's * Praife,
Whofe Merits would adorn the richeft Lays?
SAVILE! whom Wifdom views with doating Eye,
Patron of calm and decent *Liberty :*
SAVILE! to *Public Good* alone inclin'd,
The Friend of *Britain,* and of Humankind.

Would it feem Treafon, or a Lack of Wit,
To hail an able Minifter in PITT?

* Sir GEORGE.   D   To

To fay his Counfels gave a Nation Weight,
The Thunderbolt of *Eloquence* and State?
Reafon cries no, *Intention* is the Bafe
On which the Pile of *Praife* or *Shame* we place.
Should we reverfe the Medal, and portray
Thofe who prevail in Minifterial Sway,
Fit to fupply with Grace their arduous Parts,
Poffefs'd of fhining Talents, upright Hearts,
Would REASON and BRITANNIA cry out Shame,
Branding our Numbers with a venal Name?
Let us hope not—the Number is but fmall
That Councils guide, and cannot take in all:
This we may fay beyond the Reach of Doubt,
Some *Honeft* and fome *Able* muft be *out*;
Thence can we not infer, devoid of Sin,
None *Honeft* or none *Able* that are *in*.

As does *Religion*, Politics afford
More than one Way to ferve the *Sov'reign Lord*;
Poor is that Soul, in its own Notions bleft,
That, chufing one ftrait Path, damns all the reft;
As by unerring Wifdom we are taught
That the moft Perfect are not without Fault:
A noble *Emulation* may divide,
And *Honefty* be found on ev'ry Side.

Shame

Shame to *black Scandal*, *or foul-fac'd Reproach*,
Caſt at a Man on Foot, or in a Coach;
The ſpatt'ring *Bard*, whatever his Pretence,
Is but a filthy Scavenger of Senſe:
Great Minds with Pleaſure Emulation feel,
But meagre *Envy* trips at Virtue's Heel.

Let us correct, but not with Whips of Steel,
Feathers more winningly inſtruct to feel;
One Tickling leads to each defective Part,
The other, ſluicing Blood, benumbs the Heart.

Oh may the *Muſe*, debauch'd, ne'er prove ſo looſe
To ſtain herſelf with *general Abuſe*;
Impartial, may ſhe be in *Honour* bold,
Nor praiſe, nor cenſure, at the Chink of *Gold*.

Here, for myſelf, I boldly muſt declare
Againſt Ill-nature everlaſting War:
Whether in *Buſy Bodies'* whiſp'ring Tales
The carping, mean, illiberal Fiend prevails;
Whether in Friendſhip's fair Pretences dreſs'd,
She deeply wounds the unſuſpecting Breaſt,

Locks

Locks up from Poverty a fruitlefs Store
Of Triumphs in a ruthlefs Creditor;
Whether, a venal Weathercock of Time,
She fpits her Venom or in *Profe* or *Rhime*,
From me the Serpent never fhall efcape,
Tho', PROTEUS-like, fhe hourly change her Shape.
If to *immortal* FAME fhe points the Way,
And fhe alone may mine with Speed decay,
May it go with me to the peaceful Grave,
My Tomb declaring to each Fool and Knave,
That Views of Profit, Pomp, or Praife of Men,
Could never warp my Heart, nor gall my Pen.

Yet wherefore fhould I fondly fpeak of FAME,
Can Lays fo humble hope a lafting Name?
To Paftry-Cooks and Trunk-Makers a Prey,
My Works will feel precipitate Decay;
While mighty CHURCHILL's ftand erect on high,
FAME's dreadful Gibbet to Futurity.

Is there no honeft Path to lengthen Life?
Muft a fequefter'd *Mufe* engage in Strife?
Muft fhe caft off the Coynefs of a Maid,
Or fafter than a Nine-days Wonder fade?

                                        Methinks

Methinks I hear the Voice of FAME reply,
Hold, I've a darling Object in my Eye;
Let wing'd *Imagination* deck her Plumes,
And *Virtue* facrifice her beft Perfumes,
Let *Honour*, *Conqueft*, *Freedom*, all combine
To nerve each Thought, and animate each Line;
A noble Theme fhall dignify thy Lays,
And the World gladly hang on GRANBY's Praife.
Thus, Wren-like, couch'd beneath the *Eagle*'s Wing,
Tower thou may'ft aloft, and fafely fing;
While far more tuneful Songfters in their Flight,
Wanting fuch Aid, fhall fink in endlefs Night.

Proud of the Tafk, unequal to its Weight,
With glad Submiffion I attend my Fate.

Dread *War!* enthron'd upon thy fanguine Shrine,
No Touch of foft Humanity is thine:
On a rude Rock, amidft a dreary Wafte,
Is thy unhofpitable *Temple* plac'd;
Sprung from the impious Bones of murd'rous CAIN,
Gorg'd with the Carcaffes of Millions flain,
Thy *Temple*, Defolation's Magazine,
An awful! favage! and terrific Scene!

E Behold

Behold *Ambition* ſtretching blood-ſtain'd Hands,
Impatient at the rav'ning Portal ſtands;
In vain the *Widow*'s Cries, the *Orphan*'s Tears,
Or *Nature*'s Groans, aſſault thy callous Ears.
Deaf as the Raging of a boundleſs Wind,
That only proſtrate Ruin leaves behind;
Parent of Horrors! which ſtill mark thy Way,
Hateful and ſick'ning to the Eye of Day:
Fit only, like fell Monſters of the Wood,
To haunt in Deſerts, and there proul for Blood:
Lion of *Kings!* let looſe at their Command,
To ſtalk tremendous o'er each ravag'd Land.

Death, grimly frowning in nocturnal State,
Lowrs on thy Brow, Prime Miniſter of Fate:
Whether thou bidſt him ruſh in liquid Streams,
(Dire Emblems of the Light'ning's ſulph'rous Gleams)
Or wing'ſt him in the Steel's Eye-piercing Flaſh,
When truſty Blades in hardy Combat claſh;
Whether he points the bearded Jav'lin's Blow,
Or iſſues from the Poiſon-teeming Bow;
Whether, in artificial Earthquakes borne,
While Rocks lament their flinty Entrails torn,
He burſts embattled Multitudes on high,

Piercing,

Piercing, with horrid Roar, the trembling Sky:
Whether, thro' mean Blockade and Famine's Sting,
The Brave are conquer'd by this *flefhlefs King*,
Th' infatiate Monfter ftill obeys thy Call,
And, fweeping off Diftinction, levels all:
Teaching this Leffon to o'er-fwelling Pride,
That Duft and Humankind are near ally'd.

What! fays the Mifer, gloting on his Pelf,
The fhining Idol! more than fecond Self,
Won't all my Store, my countlefs Thoufands, fave
From the cold Comforts of the icy Grave?
Shall pennylefs Companions fhare the Ground
Where I am laid, with equal Honour crown'd?

How! cries the Hypocrite, with Saint-like Show,
Can't my Devotion check this mortal Foe?
Can't all the Splendor of my fparkling Eyes
Difarm his Cruelty, the *Belle* replies?

The Skeleton retorts, with hollow Tone,
Gold, Pow'r, and Beauty bend before my Throne:
One only Method can fubdue my State,
Be truly good, and I'm no longer great.

Second

Second in Pow'r *Captivity* appears,
Circled with galling Chains and chilling Fears;
More dreadful and more tort'rous to the Brave,
Than all the folemn Terrors of the Grave.
Sable Affliction's moft affecting Goad!
Painful Exiftence, Mifery's Abode!
Bane to each focial Feeling of the Heart,
PROMETHEAN VULTURE to each vital Part!
Whether we view thee in the funlefs Caves,
Where fell *Inquifitors* immure their Slaves;
Wolves of *Religion,* crown'd with hellifh Flames,
Whom bleeding Pity, fill'd with Horror, names:
Whether we find thee at the lab'ring Oar,
(Sad Monuments of arbitrary Pow'r)
Or trace thee to SIBERIA's dreary Plains,
Where painful Solitude with Exile reigns;
Exhauftlefs Fountain of corroding Care,
Thee next in Pow'r we find to *Death* and *War*.

Friends to the dreadful, the united Three,
Foes to calm Peace and fmiling *Liberty*,
Behold afpiring GAULS, in dark Debate,
Framing DÆDALIAN *Labyrinths* of State:

Fabrics

Fabrics moſt fair, and grateful to the View,
Enter not, Honeſty, without a Clue.

There vainly Oaths and Treaties plead their Cauſe,
The Faith of Nations, and their mutual Laws:
Gewgaws of Conſcience, Rattles of the Brain,
Mere Speculation, delicate and vain.
Far other Motives GALLIC *Boſoms* move,
Than the Ætherial Sparks of Patriot Love;
A lawleſs Thirſt of Univerſal Pow'r,
Still makes them wiſh, and ready to devour;
Nor heed the Means, how bloody or how dark,
So Laurels ſpring to deck their *Grand Monarque*.

Their Principles and Manners brought to View,
Behold a ſkipping, fawning, faithleſs Crew;
A *Maſquerade*, where Charaƈters are ſhown
In ev'ry outſide Likeneſs but their own:
A Tribe of Mimes, with Feathers trimm'd, and Lace,
Made up of Dancing, Chatter, and Grimace;
As *Parrots* talkative, as Peacocks vain,
Deceit and *Folly*'s motley-colour'd Train:
Such ſhines the ſad Majority of FRANCE,
Where *Virtue*'s all compriz'd in—*Complaiſance*.

F

Can

Can it be ſtrange that ſuch a Contraſt ſhould
Still thirſt for BRITISH Wealth and BRITISH Blood?
That, Slaves themſelves, they, with malignant Eye,
Behold and languiſh for our *Liberty?*
That, like th' arch Fiend, to work their ſubtle Ends,
They wiſh to ſtab us in the Shape of Friends;
Since well they know, when open Force prevails,
Their Levity muſt kick up in the Scales.

Reaſon might well expect all this, and more,
As the ſure Product of their Serpent Shore:
But for th' *Imperial Eagle*, brave and rude,
To ſtain her Glory with Ingratitude,
To aim Annoyance at the friendly KING,
Who had ſo lately plum'd her drooping Wing,
Staggers Credulity, bids Honour haſte,
And hide his Bluſhes in ſome dreary Waſte;
Since, in the Face of wond'ring Heav'n and Men,
THERESA GEORGE forgot, and DETTINGEN.

When lawleſs Depredations ſpread Alarms,
Which BRITAIN forc'd unwillingly to Arms:
When Forts were rais'd in unſuſpecting Climes,
And harmleſs Villagers, in peaceful Times,

Like

Like Sheep were fcatter'd o'er a barren Plain,
Or by the Tribe of fcalping Butchers flain:
While Wives (dead Hufbands welt'ring in their View)
Firft ferv'd the Luft of the rapacious Crew;
Then gladly facrific'd their final Breath,
So to efcape *fuch* Minifters of Death;
Who, practis'd in the favage, flaught'ring Trade,
In Cruelties refin'd their Art difplay'd.
When leagu'd with *Savages,* more virtuous far
Than thofe who plung'd them in the Gulph of War,
FRANCE rang'd in Blood whole *Provinces* along,
Horrid to tell—as mercilefs as ftrong;
Taught Ruin thro' our *Colonies* to roam,
She treated us with Blandifhments at home;
So Steel-ribb'd Dames, * with moft alluring Grace,
Smile Men to Death, and kill with an Embrace.
While her back Settlements defencelefs lay,
To uncheck'd Conquerors an eafy Prey,
AMERICA, neglected, wept in Blood,
None the *Moft Chriftian* Maffacre withftood.

Strange

---

* This Diftich alludes to the Mode of Punifhment in fome Countries, where an Iron Machine is drefs'd up in the Form of a beautiful Woman with ftretch'd out Arms, within whofe Reach the Criminal being placed, he is immediately crufh'd to Death.

Strange to be told, yet not more ſtrange than right,
Maternal ENGLAND, tho' ſhe mourn'd the Sight,
Lay totally unnerv'd, and ſlumber'd on,
Till Danger proudly dar'd her native Throne:
Till fluſh'd *Monſieurs* with Thouſands lin'd each Coaſt,
Invaſion, with reſiſtleſs Pow'r, their Boaſt;
And, may it not be told an After-Age,
May ſuch a Blot ne'er ſtain hiſtoric Page,
So much alarm'd the Guardians of our State,
That *Foreign* Aid was call'd to baffle Fate.
Oh dark Remembrance! future Glory's Foil—
Brighter to ſhow our Ocean-bounded *Iſle*.
The Sons of HESSE and HANOVER, tho' brave,
Could never BRITAIN's tott'ring *Freedom* ſave;
On our own *Heroes* muſt our State rely,
Who live to guard it, or to fail and die.

Some Armaments indeed, of gallant Show,
Were order'd forth, to ſtop th' aſpiring Foe;
Some *North*, ſome *South*, ſome *Eaſt*, ſome *Weſt* were ſail'd,
To what Effect?—each Expedition fail'd:
Ill plann'd, or ſpiritleſs, each warlike Scheme
Melted like Vapour, vaniſh'd like a Dream;

Which

Which racks, to no Effect, the tortur'd Mind,
And, like the Mountain lab'ring, leaves a Mouse behind.

At length the *Lion*, roaring from his Den,
Breath'd his rough Roar, so horrible to Men;
Rais'd his huge Mane, emblaz'd his glaring Eye,
Wav'd his fell Tail, and foam'd for Liberty:
With Fangs and Claws in terrible Array,
O'er trembling Nations took his lordly Way,
To scourge, with Sov'reign Rage, each Subject Beast
of Prey.

To show at large, and regularly trace,
The Flight of Fire-ey'd War from Place to Place,
Light by the Beams of his all-flaming Robe,
To traverse the four Quarters of the Globe;
To paint each Action, or to praise the Brave,
That conqu'ring fought on ev'ry Plain or Wave;
Thro' each Campaign successively to run,
Would want the Force and Fire of ADDISON:
Let me, content with more contracted View,
A *single* COMET's lucid Path pursue;
To show each Article in Order set,
Would make this Piece a versify'd *Gazette*:

Rough

Rough GERMAN Names would jar in ev'ry Line,
Wound each nice Ear, and clog my whole Defign;
I aim not therefore at minuter Rays,
But ftrive to give the whole collected Blaze;
Whence my dull clay-form'd Image to infpire,
PROMETHEUS-like, I'll fteal celeftial Fire.

Come MINDEN! made immortal by the Day,
When pride-fwell'd GALLIA's num'rous Hoft gave Way:
Thou glorious blood-ftain'd Theatre of FAME,
Which future Ages fhall with Tranfport name,
With thee the Æra of our Glory fix,
And wond'ring hail the conqu'ring Number SIX:
Battalions SIX! which, firm as ATLAS, ftood
Againft the thund'ring Rage of War's tremendous
    Flood,
Which durft the fierceft Shock of Fate abide,
Breaft cumb'rous Waves, repel the rapid Tide,
And fmile to fee its Foam burft vain on ev'ry Side.

Eager to make the glorious Work complete,
Burning to catch the fav'ring Smiles of Fate,
Leading our Squadrons with impatient Fire,
With all the Spirit *Glory* could infpire,

With

With all the Zeal which *Patriot* Boſoms know,
Who ſee, and wiſh to ruſh upon the Foe,
Brave GRANBY charg'd—deſpiſing *languid* Rules,
War's Pedantry—that genuine Ardor cools:
By ſlow Preciſion into Practice brought,
That knows not when Occaſion ſhould be caught.

Trembling leſt Merit ſhould aſſume her Place,
And leave her ling'ring in the martial Chace,
Fortune, with Darts of pois'nous *Envy* ſtung,
Labour'd to blaſt his Laurels as they ſprung;
Try'd what ſhe could to ſtop his conqu'ring Way,
And dim the Luſtre of that glorious Day;
In Frenzy's Rage thus *Victory* upbraids,
Hence, *Britiſh* Slave, while I protect CONTADES;
Your haughty Maſters mock my courted Pow'r,
To LOUIS I devote me from this Hour.
In Part ſhe triumph'd, but each future Field,
Taught the reluctant Sorcereſs to yield.

So in tranſlucent Regions of the Sky,
When ſpotleſs Beams would ſtrike the raviſh'd Eye,
A momentary Cloud may intervene,
And fleeting Vapour dull the lucid Scene;

Which

Which, cleaving to the Bofom of the Gale,
Leaves pure unfully'd Æther to prevail,
Celeftial Gems again attract the Sight,
And fparkling fhine with double Luftre bright.

Wide is our Field for *Fancy*'s vig'rous Wing,
Frefh Images in rich Abundance fpring;
Defcription, teeming with the crouded View,
Pants in the Chace, and labours to purfue;
While pining *Flatt'ry*, fill'd with envious Spleen,
And wond'ring Grief beholds the copious Scene,
Where matchlefs Tints in genuine Beauty blend,
That juftly fcorn fo varnifhing a Friend:
A Profpect fhe, reluctantly, muft own
By *fimple Truth* to moft Advantage fhown.

What are *Elogiums* on the *Good* and *Wife?*
Faint Tapers lab'ring to illume the Skies:
Revers'd, what are they to the *vicious Great?*
Lights to difplay the Rottennefs of State.

We need not ftraining Panegyric ufe,
A licens'd Freedom of the *Magic* Muse,

To

To conjure ALEXANDER from his Grave,
And mortify his Pride with one *more* brave:
We need not bid the mighty JULIUS come,
To fee a Race of *fresher Laurels* bloom:
We need not, fawning, give our *Theme* to Sight,
More ftain'd with Blood than SCANDERBEG in Fight;
Whofe fingle Arm, in one *romantic* Day,
So Story fays, two thoufand fwept away.

Is it impoffible to grace Command
Without a *light'ning* Eye or *thund'ring* Hand?
True Merit needs no *Foppington* Difplay,
In *Peacock* Plumes of vain *Hyperbole*;
But, like the Gems which light INDOSTAN's Mines,
With native Worth and matchlefs Radiance fhines.

To warm the Paffions, and to wound the Heart,
Why fhould we play the Scenery of Art?
Bring to aftonifh'd Optics from afar,
The glitt'ring, dreadful Pageantry of *War?*
Why wound the harrow'd Ear with harfh Alarms,
Hoarfe Drums, fhrill Trumpets, and the Clink of Arms?
Why wake each tender Feeling of the Mind,
To weep the felf-wrought Woes of Humankind;

H   To

To fwell the fullen Streams of widow'd Eyes,
To echo childlefs Parents' burfting Sighs?
Why fhow the dread Effects of rav'nous Pow'r?
Why flame the City, or fubvert the Tow'r?
Why fhould we give a melting Reader Pain,
With Streams of Blood and Mountains of the Slain?
Why picture, what the *Brave* muft weep to fee,
Thofe dauntlefs Agents of *Neceffity?*
Who, while each Breaft with patriot Ardor glows,
For *Juftice* fight—yet weep o'er dying Foes.

Glory!—bright Spark of an *Ætherial* Flame,
Humanity and thou art ftill the fame:
Megrim'd *Ambition* vainly ftrives to ape
The Beauties of thy foul-enchanting Shape;
Yet, like the painted Proftitute, can gain
Some mad Admirers to adorn her Train;
Like her too, with the Lures of gay Deceit,
The *Cormorants* of *Policy* can cheat,
Lead to Deftruction's Brink—then headlong throw
The tow'ring Fools to dreadful Depths below.

Not fo *thou* treat'ft thy votive gallant Swains,
Who court, with rough Embrace, in martial Plains;

Who

Who on the Wings of Emulation tow'r,
Free from the paltry Views of *Gain* or *Pow'r*;
Who only fhed their own or foreign Blood,
To work, by noble Means, fome *gen'ral Good*;
Who bravely ftand againft oppreffive Ill,
And but from Principles of *faving—kill.*

Faithful as chafte PENELOPE to thefe,
Undaunted by the War of Land or Seas,
Thy radiant Beams adorn each Hero's Head,
A GRANBY living, and a WOLFE when dead.

A WOLFE!—methinks I fee the pearly Tear
Stand fwelling, trembling on its chryftal Sphere;
Not fo it gufh'd, but in a rapid Tide,
That Day when *our* EPAMINONDAS died;
Like Flow'rs o'ercharg'd with Dew, you feebly bow,
And a deep Sigh remembers gallant HOWE.

More fweet than ARABY's Perfumes muft rife,
To fmiling Heav'n fuch lovely Sacrifice;
The laurell'd Shades receive it in its Flight,
While circling Cherubs fhare their fond Delight.

But

But wherefore droop? return to BRITAIN's Ifle,
And teach thy momentary Grief to fmile;
Amidft furviving Sons, fecurely reft
In SAUNDERS, MONCKTON, HAWKE, and GRANBY bleft.

Nor thefe alone—but fhould we fpeak of *All*
Who bravely follow'd at thy arduous Call;
Should we at Length recite each fev'ral Name,
We muft *monopolize* the *Lift* of FAME:
A Lift from whence, expos'd to GALLIC Eyes,
Difmay in trembling, lifelefs Form muft rife,
Chill their proud Monarch on his tott'ring Throne,
And, like MEDUSA's Head, convert to Stone.

Oft have we heard of Heroes in the Field,
Whofe Courage forc'd the conquer'd Foe to yield;
Gen'rals and *Men* adorn'd in ev'ry Senfe,
Save with the virtuous Beam *Benevolence :*
That Beam divine! without whofe cheering Ray
The darken'd Soul admits no Gleam of Day.

Where is the Merit, with rapacious Hand,
To conquer, but to defolate a Land?

To

To feed his Appetite without Controul,
Behold the Beaft of Prey rapacious proul;
Still *Inftinct* juftifies his hoftile Life,
Inftinct with *Reafon* here at mortal Strife.

Shall MAN, tho' juftly rous'd to *Self-Defence*,
(A rational, yet oft a falfe Pretence)
Without a Spark of Mercy in his Heart,
Ruthlefs perform a more than Savage Part?
Become to Humankind a lafting Curfe,
To feed his Avarice and cram his Purfe?
Not mov'd by Thirft of *Glory*, but of *Gain*,
Such Martial *Ufurers* their Rank profane;
Yet fuch have been, and fome—Oh Pain to fpeak—
Who more, if poffible, through Honour break—
Who farther yet the fhining Pelf purfue,
And rob the honeft Soldiers of their Due.

Down, Indignation—keep thy Place below,
Nor let the Tide of juft Refentment flow;
Leave with one Wifh fuch Reptiles to their Fate,
Defpis'd by *Honefty*, however great,
That of the fordid Crew it may be told,
Like CRASSUS, they, when dead, were gorg'd with Gold.

I   From

From this offensive Prospect let us fly,
And haste to one that may delight the Eye;
Behold a Portrait of uncommon Charms,
To animate and grace the BRITISH Arms;
Behold him giving Spirit full Career,
Alike untouch'd by Cruelty or Fear;
Behold his Breast with virtuous Ardor glow,
Behold him conquer and regret the Foe;
Behold him, from the sanguine Field retir'd,
With GLORY in a milder Shape inspir'd;
No proud luxurious Bashaw in Command,
Behold him cherish with a fost'ring Hand;
Behold his honest Heart and lib'ral Purse expand.
Behold him hospitable Aid afford,
By timely Largess and obliging Word;
Behold him, with a Parent's tender Eye,
View, and each practicable Want supply;
Behold him, Idol of each grateful Heart,
Unite the *Gen'ral's* and Protector's Part!
While Armies know not whether to commend,
And love the Chief, the Father, or the Friend.
Nor stops his Bounty here—behold around,
Thro' all Degrees its kind Effects are found;

Tow'ring

Tow'ring above imperfect Flesh and Blood,
It lights on all—an *univerfal Good.*
So fev'n-mouth'd NILUS, Source of Plenty, reigns
A well-tim'd Providence to thirfty Plains,
So fwell his fertile Streams o'er Mother Earth,
So give they Plenty, Peace, and Gladnefs Birth.

This Portrait, tho' imperfect, it were Shame,
Like an ill Painter, to expofe and name;
Yet fhould there one fo ignorant appear,
So much fequefter'd from the fhining Sphere,
As not to know the Likenefs we advance,
Of ALBION's Glory, and the Dread of FRANCE,
To him in Words the HERO we unfold,
Such GRANBY is, and POMPEY was of old.

Thrice happy BRITAIN! Emprefs of the Main,
May Ages blefs thee with a BRUNSWIC's Reign;
A BRUNSWIC worthy his illuftrious Race,
Of virtuous Royalty the Pride and Grace;
KING of his People's Hearts!—to Vice a Rod,
The undiffembling Servant of his GOD;
Not more with *Fame* and *public Virtue* fir'd,
Than with domeftic Harmony infpir'd.

Mark!

Mark! Grandeur, mark! and imitate the Plan,
That dignifies the *Monarch* by the *Man.*

A Brunswic form'd, as *Envy*'s Self muſt own,
To fix and dignify his native Throne;
A Brunswic on whoſe Glory-beaming Brows,
The Crown imperial double Radiance ſhows:
Not ſuch deſtructive Beams as Flames inſpire,
And wildly ſet the groaning World on Fire;
But ſuch mild Influence as, in temp'rate Skies,
The Sun celeſtial ſheds on human Eyes:
A Brunswic ſteady in his Country's Cauſe,
Firm Baſis of our *Liberty* and *Laws.*

Well for the World doth Providence provide
Such Inſtruments to check Ambition's Pride,
As wait the Signal of his Royal Hand,
Ready to guard, or to revenge his Land;
And wiſely Pow'r is lodg'd in ſuch a Heart
As cannot even *think* a Tyrant's Part;
A Heart that owns no Merit in Succeſs,
But as it gives extended Pow'r to bleſs;
That all the Pomp of *Victory* diſdains,
Unleſs when breaking proud Ambition's Chains:

Then

Then *Royalty* indeed may juftly tow'r
Stemming the Tide of Arbitrary Pow'r.

Thus mighty GEORGE fupports indulgent Sway,
While BRITONS gratefully with Pride obey.

Hear! Nations hear! nor envy while we fing,
Heav'n's choiceft Bleffings in a PATRIOT KING!

To all who hold BRITANNIA worth their Care,
(May thofe who do not ne'er her *Freedom* fhare)
This fervent Pray'r I faithfully propofe,
May all the Comforts human Nature knows,
May all the Smiles of moft indulgent Fate
Smooth to our KING th' Anxieties of State;
In the ftill Calm of a contented Soul
May filv'ring Years in long Succeffion roll;
And when—but why anticipate what *Time*
Muft bring to pafs in each Degree and Clime?
May all his Actions *Love* and *Honour* win,
Without all *Glory*, and all *Peace* within.

Religion's Minifters, may they be all
Attendant only upon Virtue's Call;

By Doctrine and Example mend their Flocks,
Nor trade for Livings as the *Jews* for Stocks:
May moral Merit make fuccefsful Way,
And with *internal* gain *external* Pay;
That, from an eafy and fufficient Store,
Blefs'd in themfelves, they may affift the Poor;
Untouch'd with furious Zeal—(a hateful Name,
That takes *Religion*'s Shape, and proves her Shame;
Breaks rudely thro' all hofpitable Bounds,
And Chriftian Harmony at once confounds)
With Charity unbounded may they reach
The faving Hand to All; and *Mercy* preach:
Correct with Tendernefs, inftruct with Smiles,
While Reformation crowns their pious Toils;
Each *Paftor* in his own contented Sphere,
To *Virtue*, as a *mitred* DRUMMOND, dear.

May *Senators*, unftain'd with *Int'reft*, feel
Their Country's Wounds, and prove the Means to heal;
Difcharge their fev'ral Trufts with *Honour* fit,
As bold, as quick, as uncorrupt as PITT.

Where tortur'd Law exalts her wrangling Voice,
May godlike *Juftice* be the gen'ral Choice;

Smile

Smile where she can, yet wear becoming Frowns,
Nor bend her Pow'r to supplicating Crowns:
May *Right*, at least, associate with the Fee,
And free-born *Juries* stand for *Liberty*;
May *Eloquence* and *Equity* unite,
As now in PRATT, to shield us and delight.

To guard imperfect Nature from Decay,
May all thy Sons, HIPPOCRATES, display
Knowledge Medicinal—and only give
The Means to make declining Patients live:
Not drain the Purse with multiplying Ills,
With fruitless Boluses and needless Pills;
But try, with learned Honesty, to save,
And cheat, like DEALTRY, the expecting Grave.

May *Commerce* ever sail thro' fav'ring Skies,
Free from th' Incumbrance of *Monopolies*;
Ne'er may her Sons, insatiate after Gold,
War's Crimson Banner hastily unfold;
Yet if again (as, Oh, too sure, I fear,
While faithless and insidious Foes are near)
Her hostile Blast should hurricane our *Isle*,
And all our present golden Hopes beguile;

If fire-breath'd *Até* fhould fuccefsful prove,
And hungry *Vultures* chace the peaceful *Dove,*
May Refolution BRITISH Councils wait,
May Probity and Wifdom guide the State
Where *Minifters* prefide—nor factious Spleen,
Incumb'ring clog the complicate Machine.

Yet wifh we not, with HERMES' flumb'rous Wand,
To clofe fuch ARGUS Eyes as watch the Land;
No, may they ever, for BRITANNIA's Sake,
Keep clearly independently awake.

When to War's *flinty Couch,* from Beds of Down,
Our Heroes hafte for Honour's deathlefs Crown,
May Zeal unfhaken brace each martial Heart,
Well to perform the executive Part;
Still may a HAWKE be found to fweep the Main,
A GRANBY to adorn th' embattled Plain.

F I N I S.